This Little Tiger book belongs to:

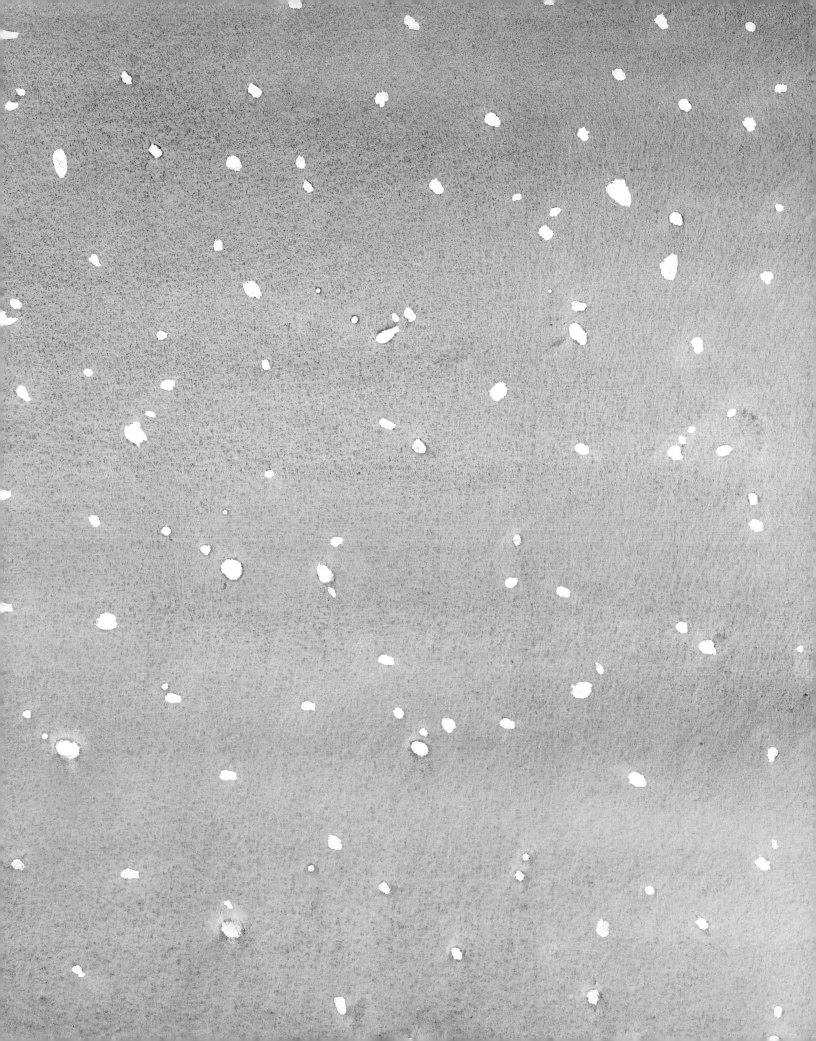

For my mother ~
who doesn't like staying
in bed either!
M.C.

For Tony Downham
G.W.

LITTLE TIGER PRESS
An imprint of Magi Publications
1 The Coda Centre, 189 Munster Road, London SW6 6AW
www.littletigerpress.com
First published in Great Britain 1996
This edition published 2004
Text copyright © Michael Coleman 1996
Illustrations copyright © Gwyneth Williamson 1996
Michael Coleman and Gwyneth Williamson have asserted their rights to be identified as
the author and illustrator of this work under the Copyright, Designs and Patents Act, 1988
A CIP catalogue record for this book is available from the British Library
All rights reserved • ISBN 1 84506 063 6 • Printed in China
3 5 7 9 10 8 6 4 2

Ridiculous!

Michael Coleman

Illustrated by Gwyneth Williamson

Little Tiger Press

London

"Ho-hum," yawned Mr Tortoise. "Winter is here."
"So it is," yawned Mrs Tortoise. "Come on,
Shelley, time for bed."

"But I don't feel sleepy yet," said Shelley.

"Ridiculous!" cried Mr Tortoise. "All tortoises
go to sleep for the winter."
"Why?" asked Shelley.
"Because it's cold outside and there's no food."

"But I don't want to go to sleep," said Shelley.
"I want to see what winter is like!"
"*Ridiculous!*" cried Mr and Mrs Tortoise together.
"Whoever heard of a tortoise outside in winter?"

Soon
Mr Tortoise
began to snore...

and not long after
that Mrs Tortoise
began to snore...

and not long after *that*, Shelley left her warm bed of leaves, and out she went through a hole in the shed to see what winter was like.

Outside the shed, Shelley blinked.
There was snow and ice everywhere, even on the
duck pond and the hill. As she lumbered along a
duck spotted her.

"A tortoise out in winter?" quacked the duck.
"*Ridiculous!*"
"No it isn't," said Shelley.
"Oh no? Then let me see you break through
the ice to get food like *I* can. Ha-quack-ha!"
"He's right," thought Shelley. "I can't do that.
I don't have a beak."

As Shelley began to walk up the hill,
she met a dog.

"A tortoise out in winter?" barked the dog.
"*Ridiculous!*"

"No it isn't," said Shelley, feeling a bit cross.

"Oh no? Then let's see you keep warm by running around like *I* can. Ha-woof-ha!"

"He's right," thought Shelley sadly. "I can't do that either."

The dog ran off after a cat, but the cat
jumped on to the branch of a tree.
She looked down at Shelley.

"A tortoise out in winter?" miaowed the cat.

"*Ridiculous!*"

"No it isn't," said Shelley, even more crossly.

"Oh no? Then let me see you run into a nice warm
house as quickly as *I* can. Ha-miaow-ha!"

"She's right," thought Shelley, shivering with cold.

"I can't run like a dog or a cat. I'm much too slow!"

The cat raced off into her house before the dog could catch her, and Shelley trudged on up to the top of the hill, where she met a bird.

"A tortoise out in winter?" cheeped the bird.
"*Ridiculous!*"
"No it isn't," snapped Shelley.
"Oh no? Then let me see you fly off home to
 cuddle up with your family like *I* can.
 Ha-cheep-ha!"
"Of course I can't fly," thought Shelley.
"I can't even hop!"

Shelley felt cold and miserable. She remembered her lovely warm bed and a tear trickled down her cheek. "They're *all* right," she thought. "A tortoise out in winter *is* ridiculous!"
Sadly she crept behind a shed where nobody could see her crying…

and slipped on a big patch of ice!
Shelley fell over backwards and began to
slide down the hill.
Faster and faster she went …

…faster than
a *dog* could run…

faster than
a *cat*…

until suddenly she
hit a bump...

and flew into the air
like a *bird*.

Wheeee!
Down she came again and landed on the
icy duck pond. She slithered towards her
hole in the shed...

but it was all covered up with ice!
"Ha-quack-ha, what did I say? Where's
your beak to break the ice with?"
The duck fell about laughing.
"I don't have a beak," thought Shelley.
"But I *do* have …

"*…a shell!*"
And tucking her head inside it,
Shelley smashed her way through the ice,
into the shed and home!

Mrs Tortoise woke up as she heard all the noise.
"You haven't been outside, have you, Shelley?"
she asked.
"Outside?" said Shelley, snuggling into bed.
"Whoever heard of a tortoise out in winter?"

And before you could say
"*Ridiculous!*"
Shelley was fast asleep.

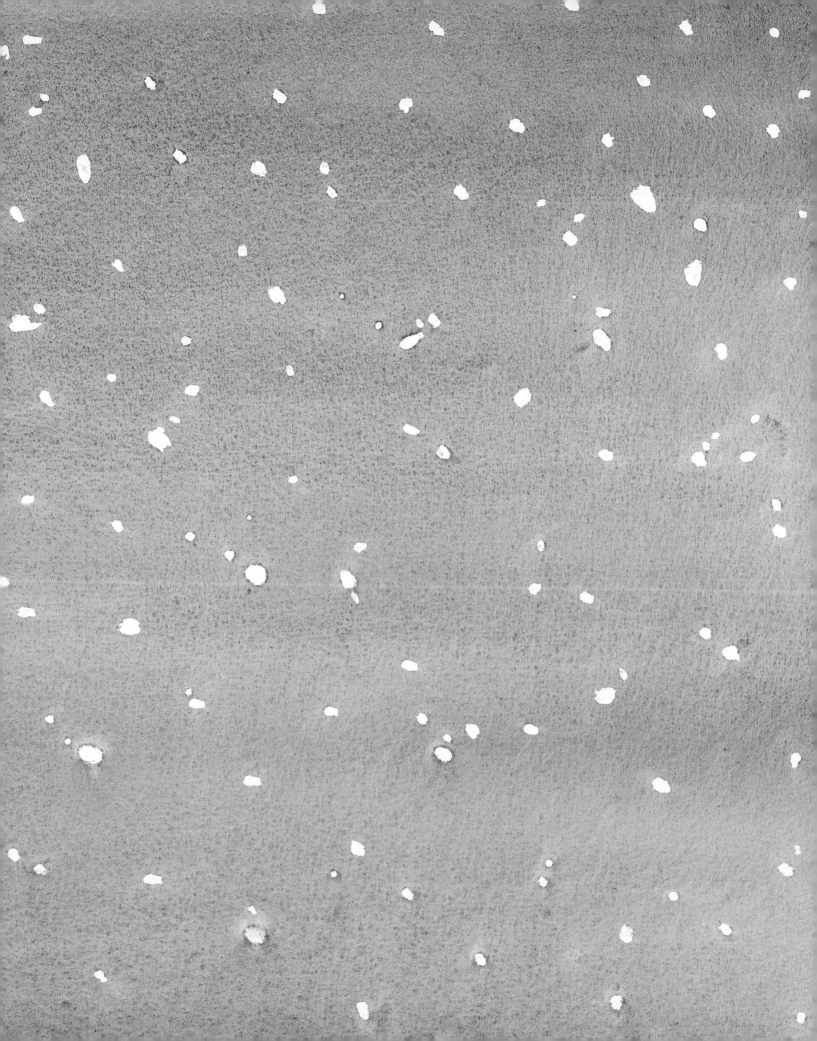

More adventures from Little Tiger Press

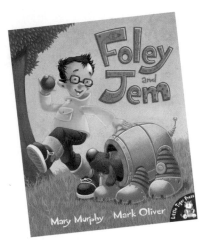

Foley and Jem

Mary Murphy · Mark Oliver

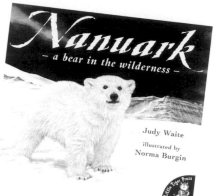

Nanuark
– a bear in the wilderness –

Judy Waite
illustrated by
Norma Burgin

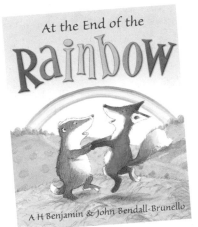

At the End of the
Rainbow

A H Benjamin & John Bendall-Brunello

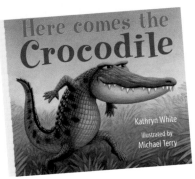

Here comes the
Crocodile

Kathryn White
Illustrated by
Michael Terry

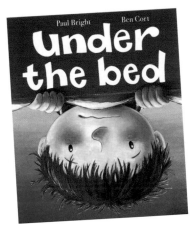

Paul Bright · Ben Cort
Under the bed

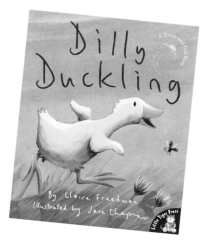

Dilly Duckling

By Claire Freedman
Illustrated by Jane Chapman

For information regarding any of the above
titles or for our catalogue, please contact us:
Little Tiger Press, 1 The Coda Centre,
189 Munster Road, London SW6 6AW
Tel: 020 7385 6333 Fax: 020 7385 7333
Email: info@littletiger.co.uk
www.littletigerpress.com